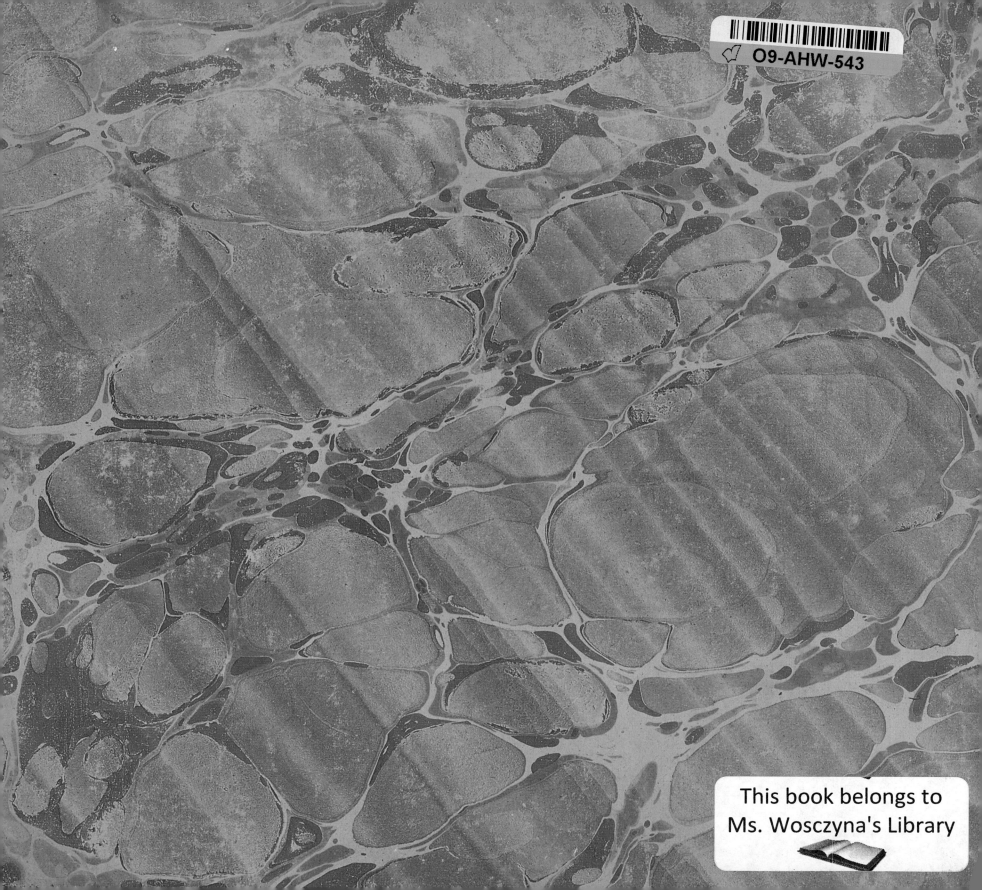

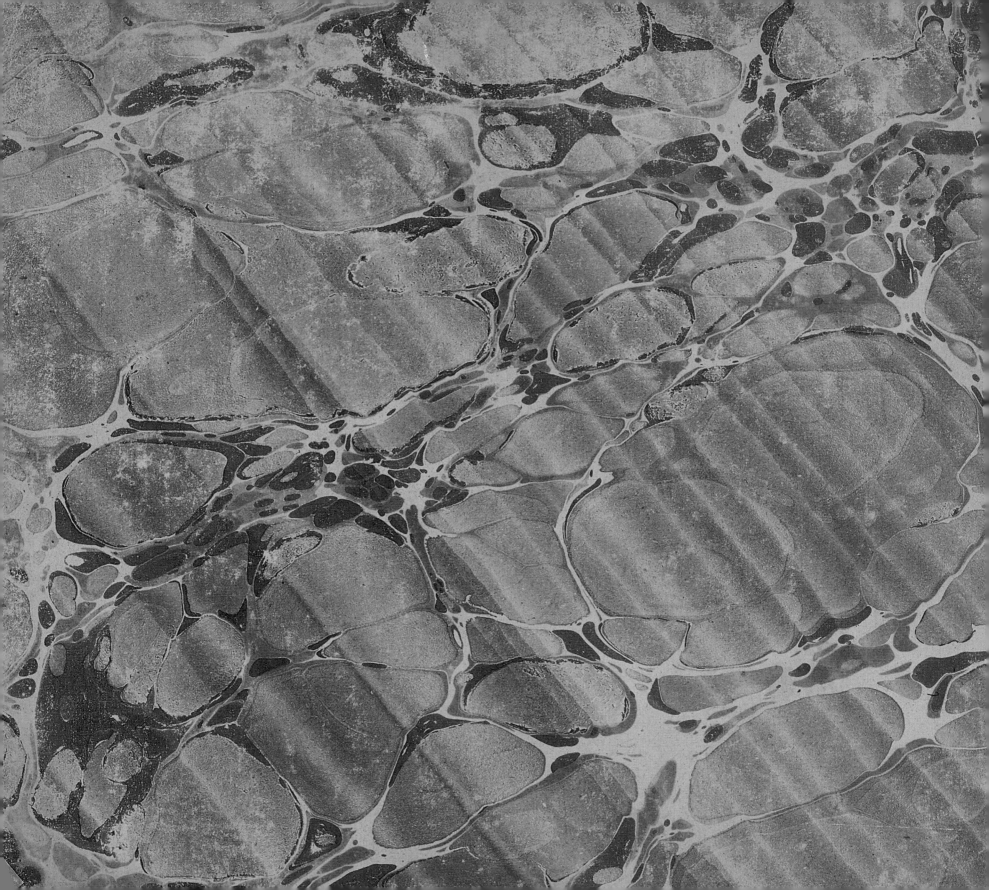

Scarecrow Pete

This story is dedicated to all the moms and dads,
grandmas and grandpas, and other family members and friends
who read to children snuggled in their laps
or curled up in their beds, as my family did for me . . .
for this is where it all begins.

And, of course, to Queenie.

—Mark

Here's to all the authors, illustrators, and dreamers
(past, present, and future) who bring these glorious books to life!

And to my dearest loves . . . my family and my friends.

—Karen

Scarecrow Pete

Written by
Mark Kimball Moulton

Illustrated by
Karen Hillard Good

IDEALS PRESS
Nashville, Tennessee

ISBN 0-8249-5151-4

Published by Ideals Press
An imprint of Ideals Publications
A division of Guideposts
535 Metroplex Drive, Suite 250
Nashville, Tennessee 37211
www.idealsbooks.com

Color separations by Precision Color Graphics, Franklin, Wisconsin

Printed and bound in Italy by LEGO

Library of Congress Cataloging-in-Publication Data

Moulton, Mark Kimball.
    Scarecrow Pete / written by Mark Kimball Moulton ; illustrated by
Karen Hillard Good.
        p. cm.
    Summary: A friendly scarecrow with a suitcase encourages a
young child to read, and together they explore such classics as
"Moby Dick" and "Alice's Adventures in Wonderland." Told in
rhyming verse.
    ISBN 0-8249-5151-4 (alk. paper)
    [1. Books and reading—Fiction. 2. Scarecrows—Fiction. 3. Stories
in rhyme.]   I. Good, Karen Hillard, ill. II. Title.
PZ8.3.M8622Sca 2005
[E]—dc22
                                                                                                            2005002485

1 3 5 7 9 10 8 6 4 2

This book is for

_____

"Why, I can go
most anywhere
by reading a
good book."

One sunny summer afternoon
as I worked in my garden,
I heard a voice say, "Hello, friend,"
and I said, "Beg your pardon?"

I looked, but there was no one else
among the squash and corn.
I thought, *Perhaps I need a rest.
I've worked since early morn!*

Pumpkin Hollow Farm

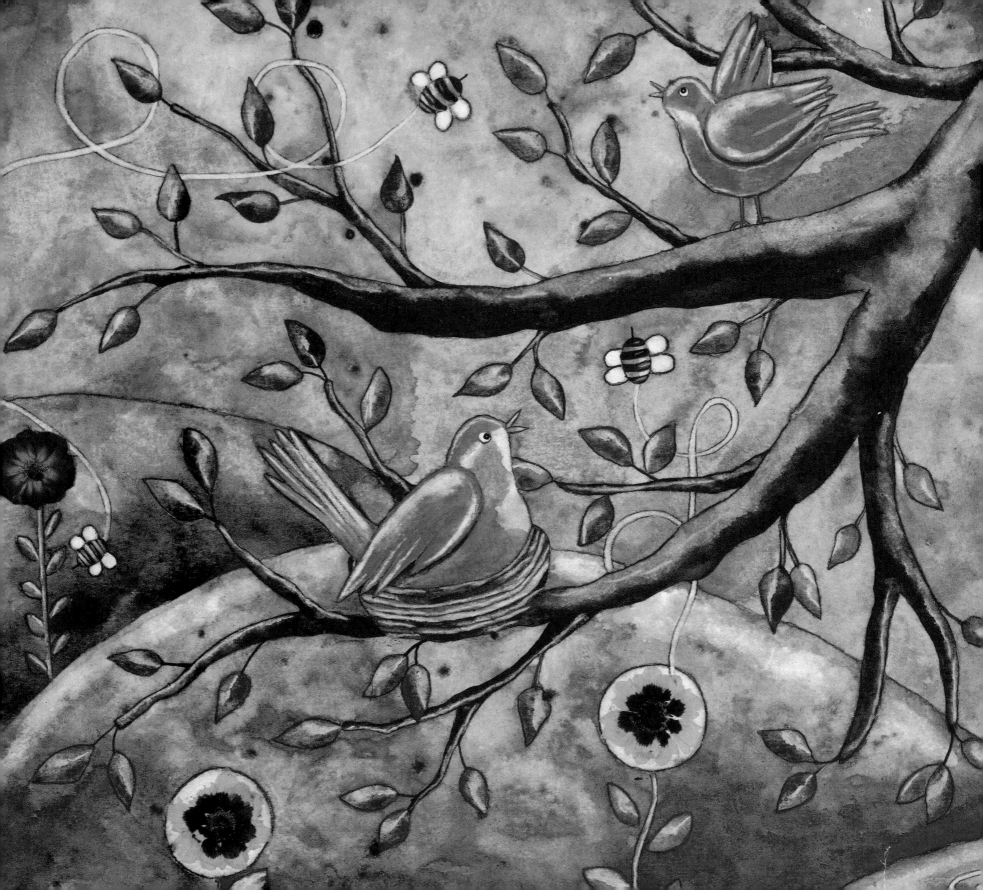

I took a sip of water from the jug I kept nearby,
then wiped my hot and dusty cheeks and sat down with a sigh.

I cupped my hands behind my head and lay back on the ground,
enjoying all of nature's peaceful, happy summer sounds.

The bluebirds sweetly twittered, joined by humming bumblebees,
while happy crickets chirped away somewhere beneath the peas.

The brook that babbled by the field skipped cheerfully along
while tickling the mossy rocks with its refreshing song.

"Oh, what a day," I murmured
as I gazed up at the sky.

"Why, yes, it is a perfect day!"

I heard
someone reply.

I jumped a mile, then spun around and searched the garden rows,
but all I saw were vegetables and last year's old scarecrow.

I peeked beneath the pumpkin leaves and combed the cauliflower.
I poked around the cabbage patch and scoured the green-bean towers.

But all I found were funny bugs
and big, fat, hoppy toads
and one enormous centipede
with forty million toes!

"Come out, come out, wherever you are!" I pleaded, loud and clear.
"Please, *please* don't tease me anymore. I know that someone's here!"

"Why, golly, I'm not teasing you," the same voice answered me.
"I'm just a little tied up here, but friendly as can be!"

"What do you mean you're all 'tied up'? Does this mean you're too busy?
Then why did you call out to me and make me think I'm dizzy?"

"Oh, heavens, no! I'd never be too busy for a friend!
I mean, I really *am* tied up! It's hard to move or bend!"

"You're kidding! Gee, what happened?
Hey, just tell me where you are.
I'll come and rescue you, my friend.
You can't be very far."

"I'm over here," I heard him say, "I'm standing in your garden."
So once again I looked around and then asked, "Beg your pardon?
There's no one here," I said to him. "I see that plain as day.
Are you still fooling me with me, sir? Where are you, now, which way?"

"Hmmmm . . . let me think . . .

"Just walk straight through the Brussels sprouts,
go past the salad greens,
then take a left before the corn
and turn right at the beans."

I followed those directions to the place he said he'd be,
but just as I'd suspected, there was no one there but me.

I stood beneath our scarecrow.
"I give up," I crossly said,
when, much to my surprise,
I heard his voice right overhead!

"You made it! Thanks for coming! Please, now won't you have a seat? I'd like to introduce myself. My name is Scarecrow Pete!"

"What? A talking scarecrow?
Boy, I've really flipped my lid!
I've never heard of such a thing.
Nope. No one ever did.

"I don't think that it's possible.
Your head's a pillowcase!
My mom stitched on those button eyes.
I drew that happy face!"

"Why, yes, and let me thank you.
I remember that fine day.
And what a most attractive smile
you gave me, by the way!"

"What? Oh. Sure. I mean . . .

"You're welcome. Glad you like it.
I just drew it on with crayon.
But really, who am I talking to—
a scarecrow or a man?"

"Well, let me ask you, does it matter
—in the long run, in the end—
as long as we are both content
to be each other's friend?"

"You're right," I said, "I guess it
really doesn't. Not one bit!"
So I climbed on a bale of hay,
deciding that I'd sit.

"Now, this is nice," said Scarecrow Pete,
"a beautiful fine day,
a brand-new friend to talk to,
and my belly full of hay."

"A brand-new friend? Do you have more?"
I asked my Scarecrow Pete.
"If you are always tied up here,
how do you ever meet?"

"That's easy—I imagine them!
I meet friends, near and far.
I close my eyes and think of them,
then poof! Why, there they are!

"I do the same to travel,"
he continued, with a look.
"Why, I can go most anywhere
by reading a good book."

"A book!" I said. "Yuck! Not for me. I read all day in school.
It's summer now. Who wants to read? I think it's for old fools!"

I felt a little awkward then and just a wee bit bad.
I hadn't meant to make him feel insulted, hurt, or sad.

I shifted on my hay bale, brushed some dust off of my shoe,
and admitted that I sometimes liked to read a little too.

"You do?" he cried, "Boy, that's just great!
Say, would you read to me?
There are several books to choose from
in the suitcase at my knee!"

That's when I saw the leather case
propped up against his pole,
with straps and tarnished buckles
and one tiny little hole.

I remembered Mom had put it there—she said it had a "look"—
but it kept blowing over, so she filled it with old books.

Frankly, Dad and I had thought it looked a little strange.
But Mom said, "Even scarecrows like to travel for a change!"

So I hopped down to open it, still feeling like a fool,
'cause I'd agreed to read a book in summer, out of school.

The case smelled slightly musty, but the books inside were dry.
I looked at Pete and thought I saw a sparkle in his eye.

"Zowie! What a treasure! Now, what book will you read first?
This is so exciting that I'm just about to burst!"

Though unconvinced, I picked a book, an epic, classic story
about a great white whale and one man's vain attempt at glory.

I brushed it off, opened it, turned past the title page,
then made a face resembling a wise, old, learned sage.

"Call me Ishmael . . ." I said as I began to read the tale—
and several chapters later, I was fighting that white whale!

Well, what I really mean is that I felt like I was there,
sailing on that whaling ship with salt-spray in my hair.
I'd never felt like this before, but that was all it took—
if reading made me feel this way, I knew that I was hooked!

We finished *Moby Dick* and then discussed it in detail,
concluding that our sympathies lay with the poor white whale.
I grabbed another book from Pete's old battered leather case,
began to read, and soon we landed in another place.

We found ourselves upon the shore of magic Neverland,
with friends named Wendy, Michael, John, and one named Peter Pan.
We rescued Tiger Lily and crossed swords with Captain Hook,
and we agreed that this would always be a favorite book.

That summer flew by quickly as we read our books each day,
with Pete upon his wooden pole, me on that bale of hay.
We cried with Laura Ingalls in her house upon the prairie
and found a secret garden with a little girl named Mary.

We met a girl from Kansas and
three friends I think you'll know—
the Lion and the Tin Man and
Pete's favorite, the Scarecrow!

We followed a white rabbit
with a pocket watch and fob
and had a conversation
with a snowman named "just Bob."

We swung on vines with Tarzan,
and we rafted with Huck Finn
and rode the East Wind as it
carried Mary Poppins in.

And after every story,
every book that we'd devour,
we'd sit back with each other,
and we'd laugh and chat for hours.

The Princess and the Pea.

THERE was once a Prince who wanted to marry a Princess; but she must be a real Princess. So he travelled round world to find one, but there always some diffic were plenty of Pr he co

Sometimes we both agreed on what the story was about. Other times we disagreed. Sometimes we were in doubt.

And sometimes we would just enjoy the book for what it was— a simple, little story written "only just because."

LITTLE IDA'S FLOWERS.

"ALL THE FLOWERS WERE DANCING GRACEFULLY WITH ON

The Adventures of
HUCKLEBERRY FINN
Tom Sawyer's Comrade
By Mark Twain

ANDERSEN'S FAIRY TALES.

THE UGLY DUCKLING.

THE HAPPY FAMILY.

But all the time, we both enjoyed each day we spent together,
reading in our garden in the warm and sunny weather.

I never will forget those days, that summer long ago,
for that was when I realized how much books can help you grow.

They teach, enchant and captivate, enlighten and cajole.
They inspire imagination and they touch your very soul!

Pete traveled on his merry way, late autumn of that year,
to pursue his dream of being a library volunteer.

It was always his ambition to encourage folks to read,
for it's the first step that it takes for someone to succeed.

We write each other every week. We're pen pals now, you see.
And that's almost as good as having my friend here with me!

I have so much to thank him for, my friend, my Scarecrow Pete.
Without his cheerful wisdom, my life would not be complete.

Scarecrow Pete
Yellowbrick Road
Oz, Kansas

P.S. I forgot to tell you abou
great King and his sword
Ex-calibur! I'll tell
you next time!
See ya!

Scarecrow P
London,
England

Scarecrow Pete
somewhere
in Africa
Mowgli says Hi!

Send to:

r Pete,
You wouldn't believe what
appened to me today! I was
about 20,000 leagues under
the sea in this amazing ship!
I just met this guy, I
he is the Captain. I'm not
him yet. Nemo is
should se
fish

Pete told
me:

Just find a place
that's comfortable—
a nice, warm,
cozy nook—
and lose yourself
among the pages
of a favorite book!"

"You can do
most anything,
meet anyone
you please,
travel anywhere
you like,
and do it all
with ease.

. . . the end.

Scarecrow Pete encourages folks of all ages to read
not only these delightful books mentioned in the story,
but any of the thousands of books published each year.

The Adventures of Huckleberry Finn, by Mark Twain
Alice's Adventures in Wonderland, by Lewis Carroll
Little House on the Prairie, by Laura Ingalls Wilder
Mary Poppins, by P. L. Travers
Moby Dick, by Herman Melville
Peter Pan, by James Matthew Barrie
The Secret Garden, by Frances Hodgson Burnett
A Snowman Named Just Bob, by Mark Kimball Moulton
Tarzan of the Apes, by Edgar Rice Burroughs
The Wonderful Wizard of Oz, by L. Frank Baum

And be sure to visit and support your local
bookstores and libraries.

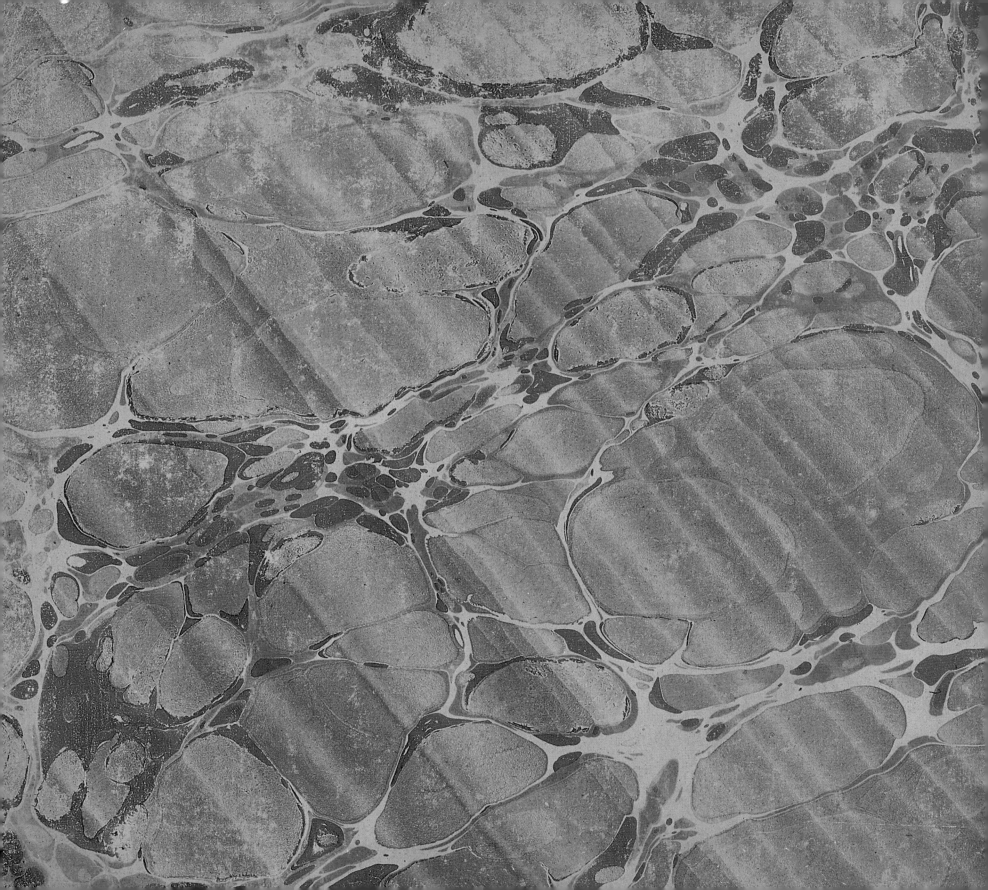